Welcome With Love

Jenni Overend

Julie Vivas

A CRANKY NELL BOOK

 Kane/Miller Book Publishers

Brooklyn, New York & La Jolla, California

We've been waiting a long time for this day, Mum, Dad, Bea, Janie and me. Mum's got pains in her tummy and that means her baby is ready to be born.

Bea and Janie are making a giant bed by the fire for Mum and the baby.

I help Mum put the baby's clothes out
onto the table. The socks are tiny enough
to fit on my thumbs.

'Tonight we'll be dressing the baby in its
new clothes, Jack,' Mum says to me.

It's hard to imagine.

I wonder if it's a boy or a girl.

I would like a brother.

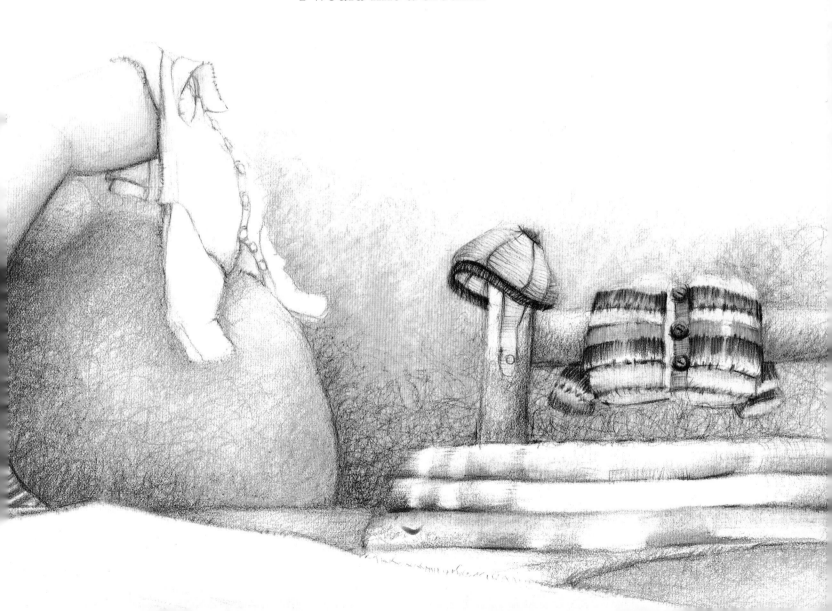

Bobbo is barking. That must be
the midwife, Anna, arriving.

It's wild outside. There's a roaring
wind and the clouds are racing madly.
I feel like racing too.

'I'm going for a walk in the wild
wind,' says Mum. 'It'll help the
baby along.'

I think if I was a baby listening
to that wind, I'd want to stay inside
Mum, floating in the warm water.

Anna is spreading all her things
out on the table.
There's a special microphone
for listening to the baby's heart,
and oxygen in case the baby needs it.

Janie is talking to Nan on the phone, telling her
that Mum is fine.

'We'll need to bring in some more wood, Jack,' Dad says.
'The room has to be really warm for a new baby.'

Our neighbour, Harry, dropped us off a load of wood last
week. He said it was a present for the baby. I thought it was a
strange present then, but I don't now.

Mum's back at last.

I tell Dad I think Mum should sit down and rest, but he says she will probably keep walking. And she does — round and round the lounge room. She stops every now and then and leans on Dad.

Auntie Meg, Mum's sister, arrives. She has a pot of soup and a bunch of yellow and orange poppies. She puts the soup by the fire and sits next to me, holding my hand.

'When will the baby come?' I ask her.

'Soon,' she says.

Bea and Janie both saw me being born, but I've never seen anyone born.

Mum has told me that she might make a lot of noise but I mustn't worry because that's what it's like when babies are born. She'll feel better if she yells and screams.

Mum's stopped walking now and is leaning on Dad by the fire, rocking from side to side. And she's right — every few minutes she yells so loudly the whole town will know we're having our baby today!

Just then the phone rings. I answer it, but
I can't hear who it is because Mum is still yelling.

I yell, 'Mum's having a baby!' as loudly as I can,
and I feel much better. The person hangs up.
I would too, if I heard that noise on the other end
of the phone.

Auntie Meg is calling me: 'Quick, quick, the
baby's head is coming!'

I kneel down near Mum and
see a round black shape between
her legs.

Mum's pushing and yelling.

Suddenly there's a little, red
scrunched-up face! I'm twisting
Bea's jumper into a knot. She doesn't
notice. She's got tears running down
her face, but she doesn't wipe
them off.

Janie is looking a bit white, and
Dad can't see the baby because he's
supporting Mum.

I watch as Anna holds the baby's
head, helping it out.

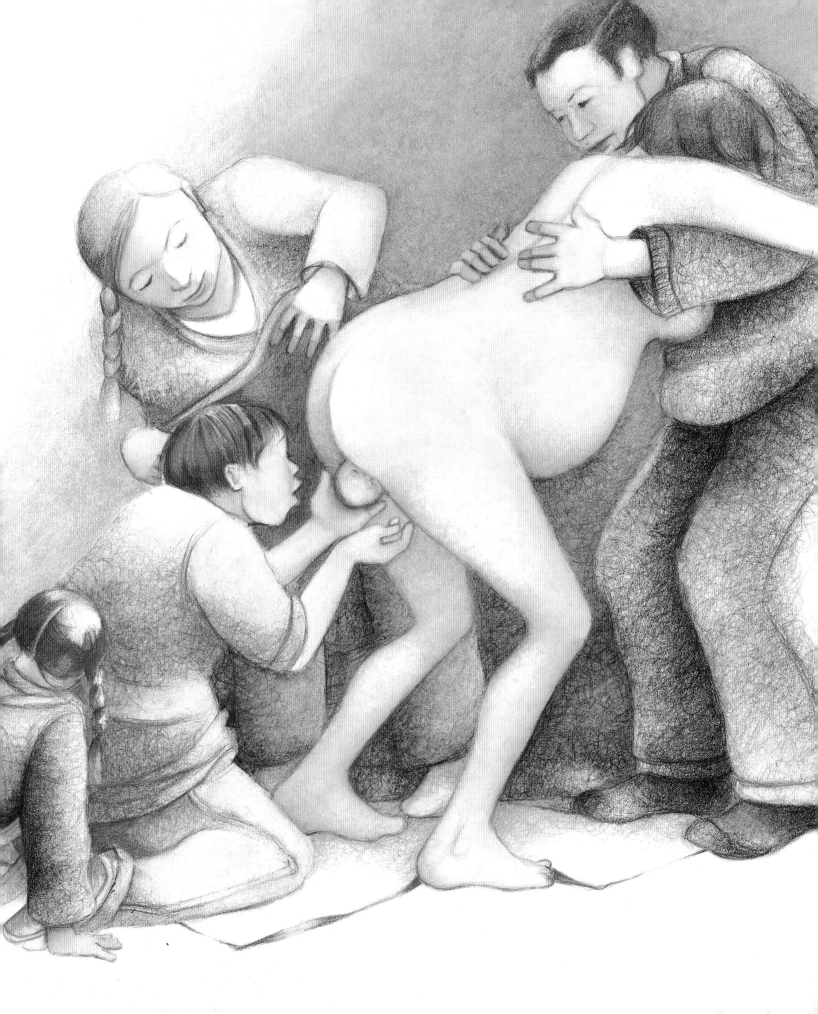

The baby slips into Anna's hands,
and she lifts the cord from around the
baby's neck, and I can see it's a boy!
    And then I hear a little sound,
like a kitten meowing.
    'Hello, baby,' I say quietly. 'Hello.'

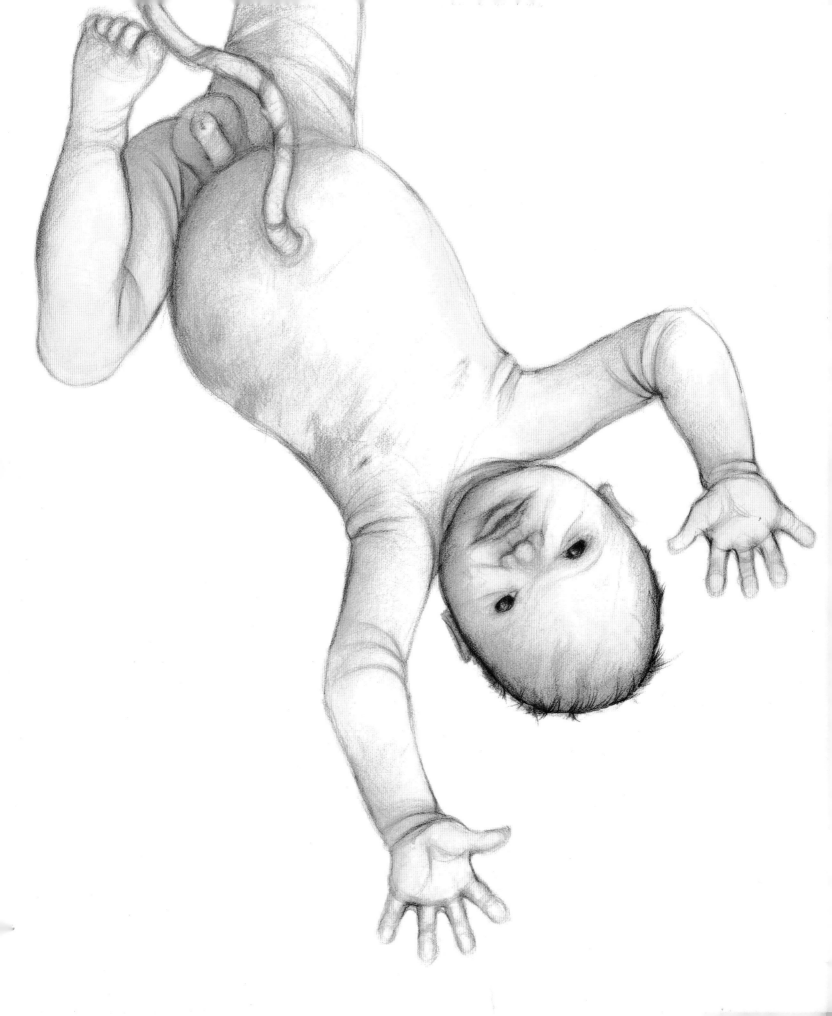

Dad is helping Mum onto the bed.
She is shaking. Dad wraps her up.

Mum lies against the cushions.

'A little boy,' Mum says, crying and smiling
at the same time. She holds him close against
her breast. Dad tucks the blanket around them.
He's crying too.

Anna gently pulls on the cord between Mum's legs and out comes a big purple and red shape.

'The placenta,' says Anna. She lays it out on a dish and looks at it carefully.

'Beautiful,' she says. 'A very healthy placenta. Lucky baby.'

'You can cut the cord now,' Anna says to Dad. He uses special strong scissors.

Mum is leaning back, watching our new baby.

'What do you think?' she says.

'Great,' I say.

Anna gently takes the baby down by the fire and dresses him.
The tiny clothes look too big.

It is very dark now and the wind has dropped. Auntie Meg
kisses Mum, and leaves. Anna gathers up all her things and
hugs Mum. 'I'll be back tomorrow,' she says.

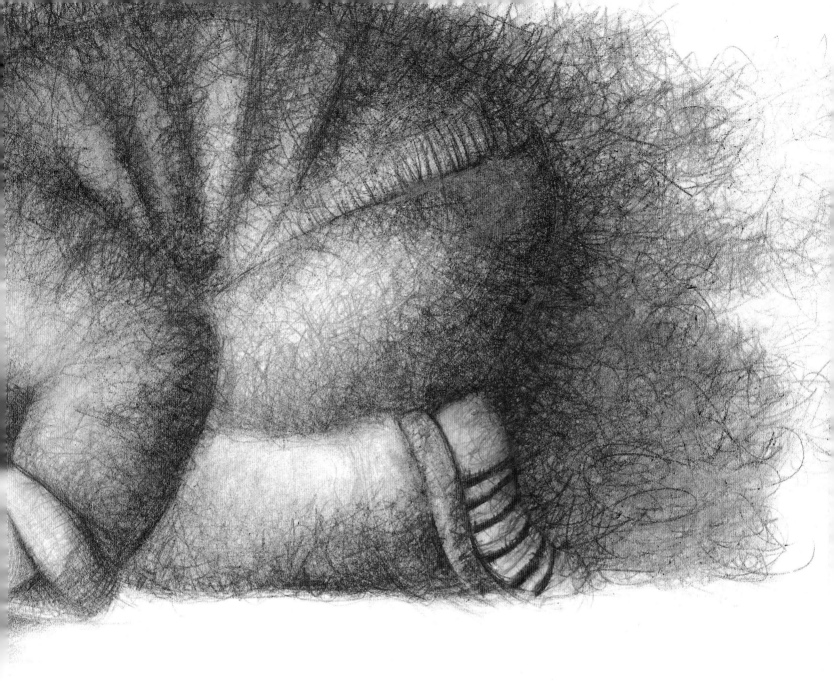

Dad gets more firewood and makes us toast and soup.

He puts on some music.

I eat in bed with Mum. She isn't hungry, but she needs a drink.

'Thirsty work, having babies,' she says to me.

Janie's getting our sleeping-bags. We're all sleeping by the fire tonight.

The music finishes. The only sound is the fire. Dad lights a night

candle on the wall.

I lie for a long time in my sleeping-bag, watching the
fire make patterns on everyone's faces.

Slowly we all stop talking. I can see the baby's head on
Mum's shoulder. He's between Mum and Dad which is
where I'd like to be.

I sneak out of my bag and hop in next to Dad.

It's warm. He cuddles me in. I bet the baby's warm too.

'Good night, baby,' I say. 'This is your first night

in the world. Good night.'

To those who inspired, encouraged,
supported and loved — thank you.
J.O.

To Alison and Betty.
J.V.

First American Edition 2000 by Kane/Miller Book Publishers
Brooklyn, New York & La Jolla, California

Originally published in Australia in 1999 under the title
Hello Baby by ABC Books for the AUSTRALIAN
BROADCASTING CORPORATION, Sydney, New South Wales

Library of Congress Cataloging-in-Publication Data

Overend, Jenni.
[Hello Baby]
Welcome with love / written by Jenni Overend;
illustrated by Julie Vivas.—1st American ed.
p. cm.
Originally published in Australia in 1999 under title:
Hello baby by ABC Books.
Summary: A family helps Mom deliver her baby at home.
[1. Birth—Fiction. 2. Babies—Fiction. 3. Family life—Fiction]
I. Vivas, Julie, ill. II. Title
PZ7.O946 We 2000 [E]—dc21 99-042219

Printed and bound in Singapore by Tien Wah Press Pte. Ltd.
1 2 3 4 5 6 7 8 9 10
ISBN 0-916291-96-0